The Magic of a
SMALL TOWN
CHRISTMAS

By Megan Alexander
Illustrated by Hiroe Nakata

ALADDIN   New York   London   Toronto   Sydney   New Delhi

My parents, Richard and Mary Shrader—who first took me to see
The Nutcracker and introduced me to the magic of Christmastime.

My Brian—who listens to every Christmas idea
and reads every draft with incredible patience.

My Chace, Catcher, and Capri—who make every day feel like it's Christmas.

Miss Sherry Bellenfant—who shares my love of the holidays and cheers me on.

My *Small Town Christmas* team—for helping me spread Christmas cheer everywhere!
Especially Karen Nagel, Hiroe Nakata, Karin Paprocki, Christina Solazzo,
Charles Humbard and UP, Matthew Kingsley,
James Kuzmich, and Amy Sapp.

And for anyone who appreciates a small town Christmas.

—M. A.

ALADDIN / An imprint of Simon & Schuster Children's Publishing Division / 1230 Avenue of the Americas, New York, New York 10020 / First Aladdin hardcover edition October 2022 / Text copyright © 2022 by Megan Alexander / Illustrations copyright © 2022 by Hiroe Nakata / Watercolor stripes by Olga_Z/iStock / All rights reserved, including the right of reproduction in whole or in part in any form. / ALADDIN and related logo are registered trademarks of Simon & Schuster, Inc. / For information about special discounts for bulk purchases, please contact Simon & Schuster Special Sales at 1-866-506-1949 or business@simonandschuster.com. / The Simon & Schuster Speakers Bureau can bring authors to your live event. For more information or to book an event contact the Simon & Schuster Speakers Bureau at 1-866-248-3049 or visit our website at www.simonspeakers.com. / Book designed by Karin Paprocki / The illustrations for this book were rendered in watercolor and ink. / The text of this book was set in Adobe Fangsong Std. / Manufactured in the United States of America 0922 PHE / 10 9 8 7 6 5 4 3 2 1 / Library of Congress Control Number 2022937529 / ISBN 978-1-6659-2980-6 (hc) / ISBN 978-1-6659-2982-0 (ebook)

Nestled under smoky hills, with skies crystal and clear,
sits my town of Heartbeat Falls, a place I hold so dear.

In spring, wildflowers bloom.

In summer,
lakes turn
turquoise blue.

And at Christmastime, it's magic
with the most exquisite view.

There's Mr. Richard's tree farm
with the piney scented air.
He grows every tree from seedlings
with tenderness and care.

At Sherry's, the town bakery,

there's gingerbread galore,

while candy canes and garlands decorate
Heartbeat's own toy store.

Bright lights adorn the houses.

Festive wreaths hang on the doors.

And over at the skating pond . . .

they're passing out the s'mores.

Candles flicker in the windows
of the church that's all aglow,

as the stars watch over Heartbeat,
joyful beacons in the snow.

Inside a mama's baking,
sugared sweetness everywhere.

Stockings hang over the fire,
hand-stitched with small town flair.

Kids glue glitter on fresh pine cones,

heartfelt jewels for the tree.

Neighbors share a meal together.

It is quite a sight to see.

Nestled under smoky hills,

with skies crystal and clear,

sits my town of Heartbeat Falls,

a place I hold so dear.

For the beauty of a small town isn't based upon its size.

It's the love shared by its people shining brightly in their eyes.

Photo by Nick Coleman Photography

THE STORY BEHIND THE STORY

I BELIEVE OUR SMALL TOWNS are the heartbeat of America. And they come to life in magical ways during the holidays.

Whether it's the large Christmas tree located in the center of the town square, the kids laughing at the local ice-skating rink, a church filled with Christmas music, or the glow of candles in the windows . . . these small town scenes are heartwarming to see and experience.

I have traveled the country for my TV show *Small Town Christmas* on UPtv, and I have experienced how so many small towns—and the people in them—celebrate Christmas in unique and special ways. From longtime local traditions to classic Christmas sights and sounds, I tried to capture an element of each of these towns and incorporate them into this book.

Heartbeat Falls may be an imaginary town, but it's my hope that when you turn the pages, you will see a little of your hometown, your local holiday traditions, and your neighbors in the words and illustrations, just as I do when I celebrate with my own family.

There's no place like home for the holidays. From my family to yours, I wish you the magic of a small town Christmas!